E
Mil   Miller, Bob
       Rumples' supper-time
       problem

MEDIALOG
Alexandria, Ky 41001

RUMPLES'
Supper-time
Problem

Written and illustrated by

Bob Miller

CHILDRENS PRESS, CHICAGO

Library of Congress Cataloging in Publication Data
Miller, Bob.
   Rumples' supper-time problem.
   (Easy reading)
   Summary: Rumples is ready to enjoy his
spaghetti with marshmallow and pickle sauce
when he is interrupted by a nasty-smelling,
but good-natured skunk.
   [1. Animals—Fiction] I. Title. II. Series.
PZ7.M6123Rv   1982   [E]   82-9522
ISBN 0-516-03637-8   AACR2

"What is that terrible smell?" cried Rumples as he was about to eat his favorite food— spaghetti with marshmallow and pickle sauce. "I can't eat my supper with a smell like THAT around!" grumbled Rumples.

"It smells like one of those confounded,
ill-mannered, short-tempered SKUNKS!"
shouted Rumples, forgetting his manners,
losing his temper, and barging from his den.

"SKAT!
SHOO!
GET OUT OF HERE!"
shouted Rumples, scaring a surprised skunk
half to death.

Then as Rumples came face to face with the good-natured, furry little skunk, he made a big mistake. Rumples breathed *in* through his *nose*. Rumples' hair stood on end, his eyes watered, and his hat cracked right down the middle.

"THAT DOES IT! Now I'm REALLY angry!
I'll get rid of that hair-standing, eye-watering,
hat-cracking smell if it's the last thing I do!"
Rumples shouted.

Then he growled and chased the frightened
skunk. . .

. . . . . . right into the waterfall.

"A nice shower will get rid of that awful skunky smell," thought Rumples. "Now I can finish my supper in peace!"

Rumples turned and walked back toward his den. He was very pleased with himself.

But the skunky smell caught up with Rumples before he had reached his front door.

"The shower did not work! And WET skunk fur smells much worse than dry skunk fur!" he said angrily.

Rumples buried his nose in the sand and tried to think of another plan.

This time Rumples chased the skunk to the top of Hurricane Mountain.

"Maybe the wind that always blows up here will blow that skunky smell away," he thought.

But just to be safe, Rumples squeezed rose-bloom perfume all over the skunk.

But nothing worked—not the shower, or the wind, or the rose-bloom perfume. Rumples' anger simmered and steamed, it baked and boiled, it roasted and toasted.

"I'll chase you and that smell to PERU, or the North Pole, or the MOON!" shouted Rumples.

"Before you do anything rash," said the kindly skunk, "Sit down and listen. I have had this problem before. I know what to do." And, taking the old piece of string that he kept in his hat for just such occasions, the skunk tied Rumples' nose shut.

"It works! The smell is gone!" cried Rumples quite happily.

21

"Now that the smell is gone, you're not such a bad fellow after all," Rumples said. "You're smart, too. I never knew that string got rid of skunky smells. Please come and have supper with me," smiled Rumples.

24

"Thank you, I have had my supper, but I would be happy to chat while you have yours." answered the skunk as they walked toward Rumples' den.

"Pull up some dirt and sit down," said Rumples as he began to eat his cold supper.

"WHAT IS THAT TERRIBLE LOOKING STUFF?" asked the skunk.

"This is my favorite food—spaghetti with marshmallow and pickle sauce," answered Rumples.

"It's awful! I can't stand to look at it!"
shouted the skunk as he dashed from the den.
"Have I lost my new friend so soon?"
wondered Rumples.

But the skunk was back in a jiffy. "I always keep a blindfold in an old stump nearby for just such occasions," said the skunk as he sat down again and began to chat.

After that, they often ate dinner together and each Christmas the two friends would exchange presents. The skunk would give Rumples a new piece of string, and Rumples would give the skunk a new blindfold—just to keep the friendship going.

About the Author

Bob Miller was born in East Hanover, New Jersey. He studied cartooning at the School of Visual Arts in New York City. A cartoonist for twenty-four years, Mr. Miller has eight children's books currently in print.

The author lives in Livingston, New Jersey with his wife Irene and son Gregory.